THESE STORIES BASED ON TRUE EVENTS WHICH WILL GIVE YOU A DIFFERENT LESSONS AT THE END

The first story

When i was a kid i lived a few blocks away from my aunt's house since it wasn't walking distance it wasn't uncommon for me to walk there on the weekends to visit my cousins, they were both girls and a little bit younger than myself and even though i was older and a boy, we still got along pretty well typically on weekends, we just hang out and watch cartoons or maybe raid the cupboard for some cereal, they always seem to have better stuff than what my mom bought, the younger of the two was the quieter one, she really didn't seem to have a lot of friends unless you count the imaginary one she always seemed to talk to, at least that's what i always chalked this up to you see it really wasn't uncommon for her to go upstairs to the attic and sit up there by herself, i never really gave it that much thought i figured that was just a normal part of adolescence to have an imaginary friend or maybe to have periods where you like solitude and just being by yourself, but every time she came down from the attic she always insisted and she sounded completely sincere when she said this that she had been spending time up there with her friend, i'd always ask her about her friend and inquire what her name was but i'd never really get a straight answer, she just gets super shy and then keep completely silent again, i always just chalk this up to one of those imaginary friend things i mean even i had an imaginary friend at one point but it was something i got over pretty quickly, but as time went on instead of getting better about this imaginary friend of hers things actually got progressively worse, what i mean by that is she didn't seem to get over it, instead she started to talk more and more about her imaginary friend after a while she even started describing what she looked like, blonde hair blue eyes the dress that she wore things like that considering how young she was, at the time i thought she had quite an incredible imagination because her description of this girl was very specific and it never really changed, it was always consistent always the same hair the same eyes the same clothing, every single time it almost became a running joke between my brothers and I, we even started teasing her about it asking her when she was gonna start getting over her imaginary friend and move on with life, in retrospect yeah it seemed kind of mean but honestly the stories that she kept sharing started to become tiresome, it was almost annoying, maybe i was being a bit harsh back then by the time i was 10 years old, we had moved to a different house and as such we didn't visit my cousins as much anymore and when we did i never brought up the imaginary friend with my cousin, i never made any mention of it, to be honest she stopped talking about it too but i think that was only because we used to tease her so badly about it, by the time i was in my early twenties my aunt had moved out of that house and into a different one and since the place was for rent and i had a lot of fond memories there i decided to move in, i want to say i had only been in there for maybe a few weeks when i started hearing banging noises coming from the attic, this wasn't something that bothered me that much and i really wasn't that concerned about it, it really wasn't uncommon for thingslike squirrels or other animals to get inside people's attics, i always figured that's what it was so i never really did much investigating unless you count going up there to put down traps or things like that, otherwise i really never spent much time in there after i'd moved in, as time went on and i got more used to the place, it actually got easier to ignore the noises but the weird thing is it seemed like the more i tried to ignore them the louder and more obnoxious they became every few weeks, i found myself going up into the attic to take out the traps and to be honest with you i could probably count on one hand the amount of times the traps actually caught something, eventually i did find out where the animals were getting in from and i was able to patch the holes and block them off, i kind of figured that would be the end of it but within the following weeks after i first patched a hole up there the noises started up again, one night after work i was laying in bed and i started to hear the banging noises again i figured i should call an exterminator in the morning so i grabbed the nearby phone book and circled one of the numbers i tore the page out of the phone book and stuck it under my phone so that way i'd remember to call them in the morning, by the time i'd laid back down in bed i noticed that the noise coming from the etiquette changed this time, it sounded like footsteps not full-grown footsteps but these were more childlike that's the best way i can describe it i guess very small and very delicate but very obvious they sounded just like a child running across the floor struggling to regain their balance like the way a toddler runs just after they learn how to walk, at this point i figured it was just a larger animal like maybe a raccoon or something but again this didn't really sound like an animal, after a few more minutes of this the footsteps sounded more frantic more hurried they went from what sounded like walking to what sounded like skipping and after a few minutes of that they started to sound like running a few moments later i heard a crashing noise coming from the attic, i quickly opened the attic door flipped on the light switch and made my climb up the stairs, by the time i could see over the top stair i saw what the crashing noise was something had knocked over a box of christmas tree ornaments and the bulbs had shattered all over the floor leaving glass everywhere, again i was thinking an animal had done this and as i said i had already planned to call an exterminator in the morning, i went back downstairs to grab a broom and dustpan and then made my way back upstairs to clean up the mess, as i began sweeping the glass up something in one of the dark corners of the attic caught my eye, it was almost like a faint blinking light flickering on and off over and over again it started out as one light and then it was two lights they glowed kind of strangely kind of like how a cat's eyes would glow when you shine a light on them, i finished sweeping up the glass and went back downstairs to grab a flashlight i made my way back up the stairs and when i shined my light into the corner where i saw the flashing light coming from, i could finally see what was making the light there in the corner of the attic was a doll as i approached it i noticed that the eyes looked like they were blinking, this freaked me out a little bit but i still decided to pick the doll up and have a closer look, when i picked the doll up and stood it upright both the eyes opened up and when i tilted the doll as if laying it down both the eyes closed, i had seen these types of dolls when i was a kid they were the kind that were supposed to look like they were sleeping when you laid them down and awake when you stood them up i kind of chuckled about this for a moment because when i looked at the way the doll was dressed as well as the eye color and hair color i noticed that this exactly matched what my cousin had described when she talked about her friend in the attic, i figured that was it mystery solved and again i had a good laugh about it , i placed the doll back down in the corner and made my way down the stairs shutting off the light and closing the attic door, before i'd even taken one step away from the door i heard something behind me, it was very faint but very distinct like a giggle or a laugh a child's laugh coming from just behind the attic door, i don't know why i did this but i slowly opened the door back up and when i looked up at the top of the stairs i saw it, two small blinking lights just like the ones i saw in the corner of the attic where the doll was only this time they were at the top of the stairs in complete darkness looking down at me, i quickly slammed and then locked the door vowing to myself never to open that door up again under any circumstance and to never go anywhere near that attic, i stayed at that house for maybe another six months before moving out and every night during those six months that banging noise continued whenever friends would come over and they'd ask me what was upstairs i'd always tell them it was storage and whenever they asked about those banging noises coming from the attic my reply was always the same, i really need to call an exterminator.

The second story

I've had a few run-ins with the paranormal this one was way different, i had just gotten out of my training and was shipped to my first duty assignment, i was living in the barracks for a while until a good friend of mine and i decided to move into an apartment away from the military post, a few months go by and he basically just moves out without saying anything leaving me with all the bills, it was a struggle but i knew i could make it happen i had to he took all of his things and i was left with the tv a small end table in my air mattress, i didn't see any point in buying anything else because i was deploying at the end of the year, i started to sleep in the living room instead of the bedroom because the tv was out there, the hallway was near the head of the mattress and i always slept with the dim light on so i could see when i got up in the morning, after a few weeks of that i started to get an uneasy feeling in my apartment along with dealing with depression financial issues and the idea of deployment you could say i was in a tough place mentally, anyways when i was a kid i had always heard of sleep paralysis and how scary it is, i never really cared i figured they were just kidding i never thought it would happen to me, boy was i wrong, it was a normal night i put on a movie benchwarmers to be exact i fell asleep the tv had a sleep timer and it turned itself off like normal i had a terrible nightmare i can't remember what it was about exactly, i just remember the horrible feelings i had from it, it woke me up well kind of i was awake but i couldn't move i felt as if i had sunk into the bed and the only thing that wasn't swallowed was my head, like any other person would have i tried to yell for help even knowing i lived alone, i was hoping and praying someone would hear me with no such luck making small noises because i couldn't yell, i kept fighting until i was able to open my eyes when i did i felt pure terror, all i could see was a black figure standing in my hallway it didn't do anything except stand there, i still wasn't able to move all i could do was look in fear i could feel it looking at me even though it didn't have any facial features, after what felt like an eternity it just kind of faded away, almost like it walked backwards towards the other bedroom that's when i slowly gained control and i was able to move my instincts told me to get the hell out of the apartment but i knew i had to do something, i ran through my apartment turning on all the lights as fast as i could, finally i got to the bedroom i crept over to the door peeking through the crack i grabbed the handle and pulled it closed, i hung across on the door i packed up a few things for the next day and i left as fast as i could, i went to work like normal i felt like i was going completely insane, so i didn't mention it to anyone when i got back home i can honestly say i was almost too afraid to go inside, i hurried up the stairs and basically kicked open the door because it was a now or never kind of thing for me, i walked in closed the door everything seemed normal nothing was out of place i went on about my day like it didn't happen falling asleep that night wasn't easy but i eventually did, i had a feeling that this wasn't the last time i would be experiencing something like this after the first time i had sleep paralysis and saw this shadow man that's what i'll call it, everything seemingly went back to normal i went to work i came home i slept okay no problem, it went on like this for a short while about three weeks after the first time i saw it again except i was wide awake this time i was sitting on my bed and watching a movie relaxing after a hard day's work i got the feeling that i wasn't alone so i slowly looked around the room and there it was standing in the hallway again but a few feet closer this time i was frozen with fear, i didn't know what to do at that point i stayed up the whole night looking around the room, that morning i couldn't wait to go to work jump ahead, a few months i had almost gotten used to seeing it every once in a while of course it still scared me half to death for a second i eventually got sick of it creeping me out so one night i yelled at it to leave me alone i live here go away or something along those lines maybe some other choice words after i passed out i woke up left the house to run some errands and when i got home it was a different story this time all of my stuff had been moved around cabinets were opened in the kitchen basically everything was moved or destroyed this was the end of my rope i packed up my things and headed to the barracks i was deploying in a week so i didn't care much jumping forward once again.

after a year-long deployment i finally returned home, physically unharmed for the most part but mentally scarred, my deployment was rough i ended up living in the barracks for a short while maybe a week or two, i eventually went back to the same apartment complex but a different building i felt okay in this one the depression had become worse along with my ptsd from combat and i ended up in an even worse place than i had been before, i left my friends kept me going though they made me come out with them pretty often i ended up meeting someone, she was great the first time i invited her to my apartment to have a movie night, she got to the door and refused to come in, she told me it wasn't anything i did it was that she could just feel things hear things and sometimes see things, she told me that my apartment wasn't safe and that i shouldn't go into it, the way she said it the fear in her eyes i could practically see her heart beating out of her chest, i decided to take her home and she said a prayer for me.

The third story

For those of you unfamiliar, snapchat is a messaging app that allows users to send pictures and videos for up to 10 seconds to each other, it's a lot of fun and is something i use on a regular basis once the photo is viewed you can't look at it again unless you screenshot the image, it was starting to get late, i was bored out of my mind watching netflix and i needed something to do, i had the brilliant idea of going on omegle, of course this led to a lot of naked men and bad ads, i was about to go find another distraction when i finally found a normal match on omegle, it was a dark room with a cute looking young woman sitting in front of her webcam, i figured it was fake and it was going to be a screamer or some prank, after an awkward silence i was about to click next when she said hello, immediately following that was the text hit me up on snapchat sa*****9, i pulled out my phone and added her just for the hell of it right, as i added her she disconnected, i sent a snap saying what's up i was just on omegle and proceeded to wait, it was around 1:30 in the morning now and i went back to watching Netflix, at 2 am i got a reply it was her it was a picture of her car followed by the text on my way baby, i simply responded with be safe lol, i then fell asleep, the next day i awake to my phone and discover the horror opening one snap at a time the first is of her driving a little weird but i don't think much of it, then things started getting real, i got more snaps of her driving one had her at a stoplight, i noticed a walmart next door to a gym the very same walmart and gym just a few minutes away from my house, so at this point i'm starting to freak out i don't really know what to do, i open another snap of her entering my neighborhood accompanied with the text get ready, the final snap is a 10 second video of her filming my house, this all happened to me last night and i've already notified the police, this seems like it could be someone in my area looking to freak people out as a prank or something but has something like this ever happened to any of you, i've never felt so scared before in my life.

The fourth story

This happened a few years ago after a rehearsal dinner for a friend's wedding, the dinner was held at a little lodge basically a metal shed in the middle of nowhere midwest, there was nothing but fields for miles in all directions, this lodge was about 15 miles away from the motel we were all staying at so we all tried our best to stay sober enough to drive back, the guy i was rooming with had one too many and was told he couldn't drive his car back but being a drunk a-hole he just slipped outside and took off in his car, around 11 pm about 30 minutes later i head back to the motel room expecting to find my roomie already sleeping instead, the motel room is empty i didn't really think much about it, i figured he had found one of the local watering holes and was having some late night fun so i went to sleep, around 3 am i get woken up to him finally walking in ,i'm ready to give him some hell about drinking so much the night before a buddy's wedding but i stop when i see him his face was white he had obviously been crying and he was shaking like a leaf, i immediately asked him what's wrong, after he had left the lodge he had taken a few wrong turns and had gotten lost down some old gravel roads, he realized it had been a mistake for him to try to drive in his drunken state so he decides to try to find some place to pull off and sleep for an hour or two, after driving for a while he saw a patch of trees in the distance with a gravel driveway leading up to it, he pulls into the driveway and sees that the patch of trees has a grown over foundation in the middle of it, he figures this would be a good place to rest so he turns his car off and closes his eyes, he wasn't sure how long he was asleep when he was woken up to a loud tapping on the driver's side window, he jumped to attention looked over and saw a woman in her mid-40s wearing a nightgown leaning over looking in his window, he thought that this woman must have been driving by and stopped to make sure he was ok so he rolled down his window to explain a situation hoping that she wouldn't call the cops, before he could say anything though the woman leaned through the open window getting so close to his face he could feel her lips on his cheek and she whispers please leave, she then stood up and started walking down the driveway toward the old foundation, he didn't think twice he started his car and reversed out of the driveway, as he was pulling onto the road he looked back down the driveway where the old foundation had been just seconds before, there was now a small farmhouse the windows were broken the exterior was bare wood as if the paint had long worn off and the roof sagged in the middle, as he tried to wrap his mind around what he was seeing, he noticed that staring at him out of a window on the second floor was the woman who had just spoken to him, he put his car and drive and floored it down random gravel roads scared out of his mind until he found the highway and made it back to the motel, he left for home the next morning i had to explain to our friends why one of the groomsmen had to leave, i just told everyone he had caught a bad flu and we don't ever talk about what happened that night.

The fifth story

In the winter of 2009, my friends and i broke into an old hospital in troy new york, it had been abandoned for years we scouted the place for weeks to prepare ourselves in case the police came, i was 21 at the time and my best friend alex was 20, we had a fascination for urban exploring and would often venture into old abandoned places, the building has four floors most of the windows were broken, there was graffiti and while you would think the place would harbor homeless people it didn't because of how exposed it was, most of the building was in an opening so it was easy to be spotted if you weren't careful, plus the building has a reputation for being haunted and most people in this area are superstitious even the hood kids stay out, so we decided to go one night after preparing ourselves with flashlights, bags, water and cameras we brought, our friend jay and my girlfriend came along as well, it was February, we parked in a residential neighborhood taking one car and we walked a mile down the road to avoid suspicion, we crawled under the perimeter fence and snuck in the shadows while the building loomed over us, there were no footprints anywhere in the snow but ours it hadn't snowed for about a month but it was still pretty cold, so as we walked in the building we were met with a long hallway with an elevator at the end, there was a staircase to our left which we took up to the second floor, it was eerie because nothing was out of place, it looked like they had just locked the place up but the second floor was different it looked like a bomb went off, moving together we realized it was noticeably colder on the second floor and it was quiet unnervingly quiet strange's troy is not a quiet city, we turned on our cameras and began asking the usual evp questions, it was then that my girlfriend said she thought she saw someone downstairs, she also kept complaining about how cold it felt, we went back downstairs and checked it out but there was no one down there, we then sat in an office for about 25 minutes talking about our exit plan when we heard a loud thud coming from the elevator shaft it sounded like the elevator had been switched on, it was eerie our research told us that there was no power in the place, soon after that sound we then heard the distinct sound of three sets of footsteps running from one end of the floor above to the other, we wasted no time as the footsteps began making their way down the stairs toward the floor we were on, we broke a window and we all jumped out, i went last just as the footsteps came racing down the hall, we all hid just in case they followed us we then heard muffled voices as the sounds of the footsteps went back up the stairs we pressed ourselves tightly against the building trying to stay out of sight ran into the shadows, it was then that my friend alex noticed there were no other footprints in the snow but ours, we quickly left, we came back two weeks later determined to find out if it was homeless people that chased us out last time this time we came armed, i had a bat in a maglite while alex and jay had knives and a bb gun that looked like a nine millimeter, the first two floors looked the same so we made our way up to the third floor, it was creepy, there was nothing up there it was completely empty and open with holes in the walls we also checked the elevators again and they definitely didn't work, we went up to the fourth floor and once again it was completely empty like the third, we went back down to the first floor feeling reassured that there was probably someone hiding out there last time but we couldn't get over how there were no other footprints in the snow but ours, as we left for home i drove by the building once again it was then that i saw three figures all in different windows on the third floor, my skin crawled we had checked that floor it was completely empty and there was nowhere to hide, we've never returned there and we never will .

The sixth story

   Growing up, i had a lot of aunts and uncles, this particular aunt and uncle were always a bit strange to me, they didn't seem to like each other very much and every time i did see them which wasn't very often, they were always fighting, apart from that their kids were kind of weird too, these were the only cousins i didn't have a good relationship with, i never really saw them very often because it seemed every few months they were moving, if i had to guess i'd say from the time i was age 6 to age 12 they had moved more than 10 times even though i really didn't get along very well with them this didn't stop me from trying in fact on a few occasions, i would ask to spend the night at their house which as i mentioned before could be any number of places since they moved around a lot at one point they actually moved into a farmhouse, there was a lot of acreage and a forest that was adjacent to it, the first day out there actually went pretty well, i didn't see my aunt and uncle much that day but i did spend a lot of time with my cousins and we were actually getting along we played video games, watched MTV, listened to music and they showed me around the house, it was actually kind of fun and i have to admit i was enjoying myself, the first night there sometime after dinner one of my cousins and i snuck into my aunt and uncle's room, she told me that she wanted to show me a secret room that was in there, this sounded really cool so i went with her, i immediately felt disappointed when she opened the closet door, she was a little bit younger than me and i tried to reiterate to her that this was simply a closet where people would store their clothing, she started to giggle and just kind of shook her head at me and said no not the closet it's inside the closet, i'll show you inside the closet and a bit to the back there was a small crawl space on the right, i watched as she climbed inside the small crawl space and then stretched out her hand as if indicating she wanted me to go with her, i've always been a bit claustrophobic so naturally i hesitated, i think that she could sense this because she came back out, i told her i didn't want to go in there if there was no light and she assured me that it was fine all you had to do was feel your way around, at this point i started asking questions mostly because i was a bit nervous stuff like how far back does it go and what's inside there, she told me that it went back quite a ways and that she wasn't sure what was inside of it because she never took a light with her, she just kind of felt her way around the one thing that she did mention that struck me as kind of creepy was that as you went back it would start to feel like you were going down a hole, i guess architecturally this really didn't make any sense, i mean why would there be a hole inside a crawl space in a closet, what could that possibly be used for, after a few moments of this conversation she went back inside the crawl space and said there's nothing to be afraid of i'll go inside first and show you and then i'll come back out then you and i can go in together okay ? for some stupid reason i actually agreed to this and i watched and listened as she went inside the crawl space and seemed to vanish into the darkness, it seemed like she was in there for a long time but in reality it was probably only a few minutes, she peeked her head out the crawl space entrance and said come on and reluctantly i went inside with her, the crawl space was extremely small quite narrow in fact we had to be on our hands and knees to get through it literally crawling, as we went i had only gone a few feet before we were crawling in complete blackness, as i mentioned i'm highly claustrophobic and i was beginning to have a bit of a panic attack, i couldn't see anything and the only way i knew my cousin was still in front of me is every couple of seconds i would reach out and tap the bottom of her foot just to make sure she was still there, the air inside was extremely dusty and i started to cough, i had only been inside a few moments and i decided i had enough, i had made up my mind and i backed out of the crawl space, the rest of the night she didn't talk to me, i think in a way i'd kind of let her down, she probably expected me to be super brave or something like that but to be perfectly honest with you i was terrified not just because it was claustrophobic but there was something about the darkness there that just didn't sit well with me something inside that crawl space didn't feel right, i couldn't put my finger on it but

but i didn't want to spend another moment in there, i just felt like i had to leave something inside my head was telling me to get out and i wasn't about to ignore it, the next morning my cousin was kind of teasing me about the whole thing calling me a fraidy cat and saying that she didn't know boys were afraid of the dark, yeah this made me mad of course it did, i mean she was seven years old and calling me a coward how could i not be upset by this, it's gonna sound really immature but i got sick of being teased, i got mad at her i just wanted her to stop calling me a coward and i told her i was gonna prove to her that i wasn't afraid, i decided to go back up to the closet and go back into the crawl space by myself, i told myself that if she could go in there alone then so could i and that's exactly what i did, we went back up to the closet and she stood outside as i made my way slowly into the crawl space and started to crawl on my hands and knees to the right i had only been in there for a few seconds and my heart was already in my throat, nothing seemed to be calming my nerves, my fingernails were practically digging into the wooden planks beneath my hands, i was starting to sweat and not because it was hot in there but because i was terrified despite this i kept moving after about a minute or two of crawling it dawned on me just how far back this crawl space actually went, i didn't have a light with me or anything like that so i couldn't see which direction i was going or what exactly i was touching i just kept feeling in front of me hoping that i didn't fall down any holes or shafts, after a few more tense moments, i could feel what she was talking about when she described this hole an incline in the floor, that didn't seem to make sense, i made my way slowly down the incline which only seemed to grow steeper the further in i went, the incline started to become so steep that i had to push my hands backwards to stop myself from sliding on the dusty planks, i remember calling out over my shoulder to my cousin asking her how much further i had to go but she didn't reply i couldn't even hear her now, i'm not sure if it's because the sound was dampened that heavily or if she wasn't outside the closet anymore, the only sounds that became obvious at this point was my breathing and my still accelerated heartbeat, it was at this moment that something made me come to a dead stop, i could feel a rush of cold air near my hand, it just felt like icy air going across my fingertips and nowhere else i was thinking that perhaps this was a draft or that maybe i was getting close to a ventilation shaft that wasn't sealed properly and that was when i felt it something cold splashing on my fingers, the first thought i had was that there was a leak in the roof and that this was just water but the thing is it hadn't rained for several days when i touched the liquid with my other hand it didn't feel like water, it felt almost slimy and it was also a bit sticky and as i raised my hand up to my face whatever this stuff was it smelled rotten spoiled maybe even a bit moldy, i was just about to put my hand back down and continue crawling when i felt something touch my other hand there was no mistaking what it was, i was feeling fingers cold and clammy fingers digging into my skin, as quickly as i could i backed my way out doing my best not to scream, when i got out of the crawl space and looked around i couldn't see my cousin, i ran back down the stairs and found her in the living room watching tv, i must have looked awful because when she saw me she asked me if i was sick, i asked her to tell me what was inside that crawl space and she got a very puzzled look on her face, she said why did something happen, about an hour later my aunt and uncle came home and i asked them if they could take me back to my parents house which they did, i never spoke to my parents about this event or my aunt and uncle and i never discussed it with my cousins either, as per usual my aunt and uncle ended up moving house a few months later, i never could find a rational or logical way to explain this event and i am absolutely not making this up, this really happened to me my only regret is that no one else experienced it with me and i have absolutely no evidence to support it but this is one hundred percent true this really did happen and i absolutely wish that it hadn't .

The seventh story

A few years ago, i was working as a gas station attendant at an heb in a suburban town neighboring houston texas, i had been working there for a few months at the time of this occurrence, anyway one day i'm working around six or seven pm when i get a sudden rush of customers after a long period of no activity and most are paying with cash, this is not uncommon working at a gas station at least not in my area, once i get through about 15 or 20 customers that had lined up things calmed down, even so i keep watch on the customers mostly to make sure nobody stole anything anything stolen during my shift would likely come out of my paycheck, at about this time a beat-up truck comes speeding up to the station slams on the brakes and nearly runs into my kiosk, he parks very sloppily dead, in the center of all the action outsteps a pale lanky man in a wife beater and grungy jeans covered in tattoos, he almost runs up to my kiosk at this point i know to myself that the man's tattoos are neo-nazi tattoos eagles lightning ss symbols swastikas the works doing my job, i ask him how i can help him, he doesn't want gas doesn't want cigarettes doesn't want food he wants to use the bathroom and wants as much cleaning supplies as i can spare paper towels soap he specifically mentions cleaning chemicals, i notice he has some reddish stains on his hands and forearms, i tell him he can go over to the main store to go to the bathroom, i give him some paper towels and nothing more as he goes back to his truck, i watch him closely he seems very nervous to me and is almost frantically cleaning himself in the inside of his car as as best he can, at this point i called the main store to report the suspicious behavior but they're not helpful, i notice at this point that his passenger window has been more or less shattered and he's pushing the many remaining shards out of his car and onto the pavement, i see that he sees me on the phone almost immediately he gets the car going and drives off but stops in the parking lot he's there for less than a minute and then speeds off, it's getting dark at this point i want to investigate more or call the store again but i get another wave or two of customers and my hands are tied, about an hour later i finally get a chance to clean up the giant massive shattered window the guy left for me, upon closer inspection of the shards i find large clumps of black curly hair amongst the debris, they appear to be from someone's scalp and they appear to have blood on them, i get some latex gloves from the kiosk put them on and use them to pick up the hair clumps and put them in a bag like something out of csi, i called the main store again with the news and my supervisor doesn't seem particularly concerned, at the end of my shift i turn the evidence over to my boss and he says he'll take care of it, a few days later i checked with my boss to see what happened with the evidence he said the police weren't going to investigate go figure.

The eighth story

This happened around four years ago when my car had broken down and i had to walk to work, i was working second shift at the time and that meant walking home at around midnight every night, this really didn't bother me because the city was fairly safe i lived in the kind of city where it was routine for the police to go up and down the business districts and check the locks on all the doors, again it was an extremely safe city almost nothing bad ever happened there, this was late October or early November and the temperatures were starting to drop on a couple of occasions when i was walking home we even had freezing rain i unfortunately had the bad habit of never properly dressing for the weather because i never was the kind to plan ahead so as such i tried to get home as quickly as possible every night, one night on my way home it was particularly cold and i was only wearing a spring jacket i was getting pretty good at navigating the city on foot, at this point i figured i could save about 15 minutes by cutting through a semi-wooded area it really didn't seem like a bad idea at the time and i certainly didn't think it was dangerous for me to do it, i figured worst case scenario would be i'd trip and sprain my ankle or something like that but again i was freezing and i just wanted to get home so the thoughts of anything more dangerous than that really didn't enter my mind, after just a few minutes i had worked my way through the wooded area and i could see pavement up ahead which meant that i had found my way back to the road my sneakers had barely touched touched the pavement when i saw headlights approaching, i of course thought nothing of this and continued walking within about 45 seconds i could see that the vehicle that was approaching behind me appeared to be some sort of a tow truck it was extremely rusty and very old like something you'd see on a black and white tv show, at first i thought it might be one of the work trucks from one of the local garages but as it drove past me i didn't see any decals on the side that i recognized the truck had gotten about 15 or 20 feet ahead of me when it slammed on its brakes and i don't mean it slowed down i mean the truck just came to a dead stop, to be honest this did make me a little bit nervous but i tried to ignore it and just continued walking as i was just about to pass the truck i saw the driver roll the window down and flick a cigarette butt out onto the road the driver then stuck his head out the window and called out to me saying something like hey you, i pretended not to hear him and kept walking and then he hit the horn my head quickly snapped around and i said yes can i help you the driver then exited the vehicle and walked towards me when he got within a couple of feet of me the first thing i noticed was that he stunk he smelled like booze and his eyes appeared to be extremely glassy and bloodshot ,he looked me dead in the eyes and then pointed at the area where i exited the tree line he then said do you know that you were trespassing, i said no i'm sorry i had no idea, he suddenly looked incredibly angry he got about three inches from my face and said don't lie to me at this point i was completely freaking out, something about this guy just seemed off and i had this strange feeling that he wasn't the property owner, my heart was pounding in my chest and i could feel my adrenaline coursing, the sensation was so strong that i might throw up without hesitating, i started to run i got off the road and made my way back for the tree line when i hear the door of the truck slammed shut and the vehicle start to accelerate, i backtracked through the woods and made my way back to one of the city streets at this point i was fairly confident that i had lost him, my adrenaline wasn't pumping as badly anymore and i had calmed down, significantly i started making my way back home minus the shortcut i want to tell you that this is where this story ends but it's not by the time, i was about three blocks from home i see the exact same tow truck come speeding through one of the red lights in front of me and come to a sudden screeching halt not more than 15 feet away it was like something out of a horror movie, how could this guy possibly know where i was going there is no way in hell he could have followed me, i kept telling myself that this is not happening i see this guy exit his truck and start walking towards me i had just started to run when a police car suddenly pulls up and turns on its lights, apparently the officer had been parked in a parking lot across the street to monitor traffic when he saw this guy go through the red light while the police officer was questioning him i ran up to him and told him what had happened that the guy had been following me, i later found out that the guy was under the influence of alcohol as well as narcotics and that not only did he not own the land that i had crossed through he didn't even live in that city, he also suffered from some sort of mental illness and he had a criminal history, i definitely learned my lesson that night one don't take shortcuts home it may not end in your favor, two don't trespass don't ever it's honestly not worth it you never know who you might run into .

The ninth story

When i was about 13 my parents and i moved to an old house, it was at least 90 years old but it was large and in pretty good condition for a house that old, i was an only child i got the second biggest room on the second floor and that room was huge, sometimes my parents left me at home by myself for a few hours whether they were going shopping or on a date, i always asked to stay at home i didn't mind staying at home because i'd like to think of myself as responsible and trustworthy it made me feel special, one night at around 6 pm or so, my parents had to go run some errands, they were the kind of people who spent long hours out shopping for the best deals and they used a lot of coupons on whatever they could and i didn't want to be involved in this at all so i decided not to come, i stayed in my room and watched some tv then at around 8pm i got hungry and decided to get a snack, now at this point the house is very dark so i grab my cell phone and use it as best as i can to light up the hallway since the hallway didn't have a light, now this was before cell phones had built-in flashlights so i just used all the light my screen could give until i made it to the kitchen, the kitchen light had been left on by my parents, i put my phone on the counter, as i was walking to the pantry i saw a man hunched down in the corner by the back door, he was wearing black and red clothing and he had long greasy unkempt hair, i didn't see his face because his head was facing the wall, he was holding a large knife and he didn't notice that i had spotted him, i wanted to scream but i used my hand to cover my mouth and walked back upstairs leaving my cell phone down there, i was not walking over to get it we didn't have any phones upstairs, so i walked into my room locked the door and i hid in my closet, i start crying silently and start thinking the worst, he was going to find me and kill me i just knew it, then i heard someone coming up the stairs i felt sick and i had never been so afraid in all my life, then i heard someone open the door to my parents room which was two rooms away from mine, i then hear police sirens outside and i hear the door being knocked on, i breathe a sigh of relief, i hear the man running back down the stairs quickly and he's trying to open our back door then i hear our front door being pushed down and i heard footsteps of two people coming upstairs and they start searching our home, the police come to my room and let me know it's safe so i opened the door, i later found out that our neighbors saw this man unlocking our back door with a key and saw that he had a knife and called the police, my parents arrived a few minutes later and my mom started hugging me and crying, the man unfortunately escaped, i cried and cried and i got no sleep that night because the man had a key we changed the lock but we eventually moved way out of state, i'm 23 now i have moved past it but there are several questions i still have how did he get a key, why did he want to come to our house and what would he have done if the police showed up any later .

The tenth story

In the city where i live there's an old water tower at the top of a hill near one of the parks, the water tower itself hasn't been used for more than 50 years so it just kind of sits dormant, let me try to describe what the building looks like, it's sort of a cylinder shape not unlike a coliseum and there are tons of alcoves and archways on it the entire perimeter is surrounded by a fence and as you would expect there's also tons of no trespassing signs posted everywhere there is electricity going to the site because at night the sodium lights on the building light up but from the road they're almost invisible and that's due to the fact that the entire site is completely surrounded by trees that have grown so thick and tall over the years that from the road the building itself is almost completely invisible, the place had fascinated me ever since i was a kid, i always told my parents that i wanted to go there and just see what it looked like up close but they always warned me that it was on private property and that it was clearly marked that you could not enter the site since i was just a child, at the time i of course respected my parents wishes but that all changed when i turned 20 years old and i was no longer living with my parents, i got the crazy idea one night that i was gonna go up to the water tower jump the fence and just have a look around, just kind of explore the property you know i want to state right now that i do not condone this type of activity, this behavior is entirely deplorable and it's also illegal and you definitely should not do it and maybe by the time i get to the end of this story you'll agree 100 percent with what i'm saying and you'll understand clearly why i'm saying it, anyway i think it was a Wednesday night or maybe a Thursday night, not that that really makes a difference but the reason i chose a midweek night was because i had a feeling that on the weekend it was highly possible that teenagers would go there to try to drink thinking that the place was secluded enough that they wouldn't get caught in my 20 year old mind this seemed like sound reasoning, so i took that chance i guess in a way it was just kind of selfish reasoning, i wanted to enjoy this experience alone and i didn't want anyone to spoil it for me and on this particular night i did exactly what i said i was going to do, i went to the site around 10 o'clock and i jumped the fence my first impressions were a bit underwhelming, i don't know what exactly i was hoping to see but in my mind i just pictured it being different maybe more creepy maybe better lit i'm not really sure, i just pictured it being different the lighting really wasn't that great there again the place was illuminated by sodium lights but they were old very yellow and very dim, a few of them were even burned out, the good news about this was that it gave me lots of shadows to hide in, the bad news was i didn't bring a flashlight with me that night so i had to be extra careful where i was walking i didn't want to trip and hurt myself, this was before cell phones became a really popular thing so if i did get some sort of an injury like a broken leg, i was screwed, i hadn't been on the site for more than two or three minutes when i started hearing voices naturally the first thing in my mind goes right back to what i said about teenagers looking for a place to drink, i thought maybe they were getting an early start on the weekend or something like that but the more i listened to the voices the more i realized that these weren't teenagers the voices were much deeper more mature and had kind of a gravelly tone to them, my best guess was that these people were most likely middle aged, i probably should have taken that as my cue to get out of there but i got kind of curious and i slowly made my way through the shadows to where the voices were coming from, after only a few moments i could finally see where the voices were coming from imagine my surprise when i saw four figures standing about 40 feet away from me, inside of the fence line they were far enough away and speaking quietly enough that i couldn't really understand the extent of their conversation but i did pick up on a few key words that stood out to me, one of them was the word money and the other was the word stuff even though these four individuals were quite a distance from me, there was just enough lighting that i could see money exchanging hands as well as some bags it was at that moment that it hit me that i was witnessing a drug deal, i did my best to stay quiet as i slowly worked my way back to the area that i had jumped the fence at this point my heart was beating a million miles an hour and i started panicking as soon as i got what i thought was a safe distance from them, i did my best to jump the fence in one clean move but my shoelace got hooked causing me to hit the ground with a thud as well as shake the whole fence, i immediately picked myself up and started running and what happened next still gives me nightmares, i can hear shouting behind me and two distinct pops as bullets whizz past me while i'm running, at that age i was actually a pretty fast runner so i booked it for home as quickly as i could, i'd like to tell you that i called the police and that they caught these four guys but that's not what happened i didn't call the police i was afraid of getting fined for trespassing or possibly even arrested, i just thank god that i didn't get killed that night because the probability of that was extremely high, so here's my advice to anyone that's into things like urban exploration if it's private property please just stay out i absolutely could have gotten in trouble with the law for what i did that night but i also could have lost my life i want you to think about that .

The end ...

Printed in Great Britain
by Amazon